Zoom Squirrel

Zing Squirrel

Flappy Squirrel

Norman

Quiz Squirrel

Nutshell
(Squirrel to the Stars)

Wink Squirrel

Klink Squirrel

I **star** in
part of
this book!

UNLIMITED SQUIRRELS in
I Want to
Sleep Under
the Stars!

Wowie!

Zowie!

By Mo Willems

Let's **read** it!

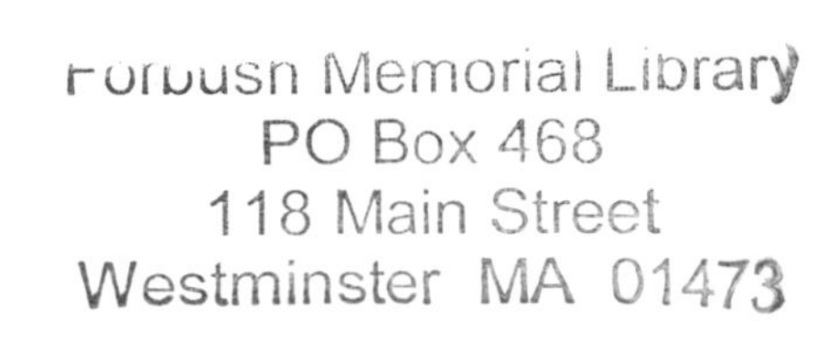

For Sara Simmons!

Look, **Zip Squirrel**!
I made a
Table of Condiments!

Thanks, **Klink Squirrel**!
But I wanted a
Table of Contents!

TABLE OF CONTENTS

HAPPY

EXCITED

CONFUSED

ENCOURAGING

FRUSTRATED

SURPRISED

MAD

DETERMINED

FUNNY

Look for the **EMOTE-ACORNS** in this story. They pop up when the Squirrels have **BIG** feelings!

The BIG Story!

I Want to Sleep Under the Stars!

By Mo Willems

Hi, **Zoom Squirrel**!

Did you say you want to **sleep** under the stars?

Yes, **Zip Squirrel**.

I like the **stars**.

I love the
peace and **quiet**.

I have **never** slept under the stars before.

It is my **dream**.

SQUIRREL FRIENDS!

Yes?
Hi!
What's up?
You called?
Hello!

Zoom Squirrel wants to sleep under the stars for the **first time**!

Wow.

We must **help**!
Cool.

How?

When I try
something new,
I like to be
encouraged.

"**En-cour-aged**"?
What does
that mean?

Being told
you can do it
by a friend!

Being **encouraged** gives me **courage**!
What are we waiting for, **Squirrels**?

LET'S ENCOURAGE
ZOOM SQUIRREL!

GO, ZOOMY!
GO, ZOOMY!
GO, ZOOMY!

YOU CAN DO IT!

SLEEP!
SLEEP!

SLEEP!

PLEASE
STOP!

What is **wrong**?
We want to **encourage** you.

I **do not want**
to be encouraged.

I want PEACE and QUIET!

Oh.
PEACE
and

QUIET.
Got
it.

We will be
Team PEACE!

We will be
Team QUIET!

Zip!
Zip!
Zip!

Zap!
Zap!
?
Zap!

PEACE!
PEACE!
PEACE!

Quiet!
Quiet!
Quiet!

PEACE!
Quiet!
Quiet!

PEACE!
PEACE!
Q
Quiet!

SQUIRREL FRIENDS!

I know you are trying to **help** me sleep under the stars. . . .

But it is
not working.

How do you know?
Well,
I am
awake. . . .
And . . .

THE STARS

ARE GONE!

It is **too late** for this Squirrel.
Or is it
too early?

WAIT!

This is a **Squirrel problem**!

We will find a **Squirrel solution**!

SQUIRRELS AWAY!

Well, I—

YAWN

—learned something tonight.

Squirrels do **not**
know much about
sleeping . . .

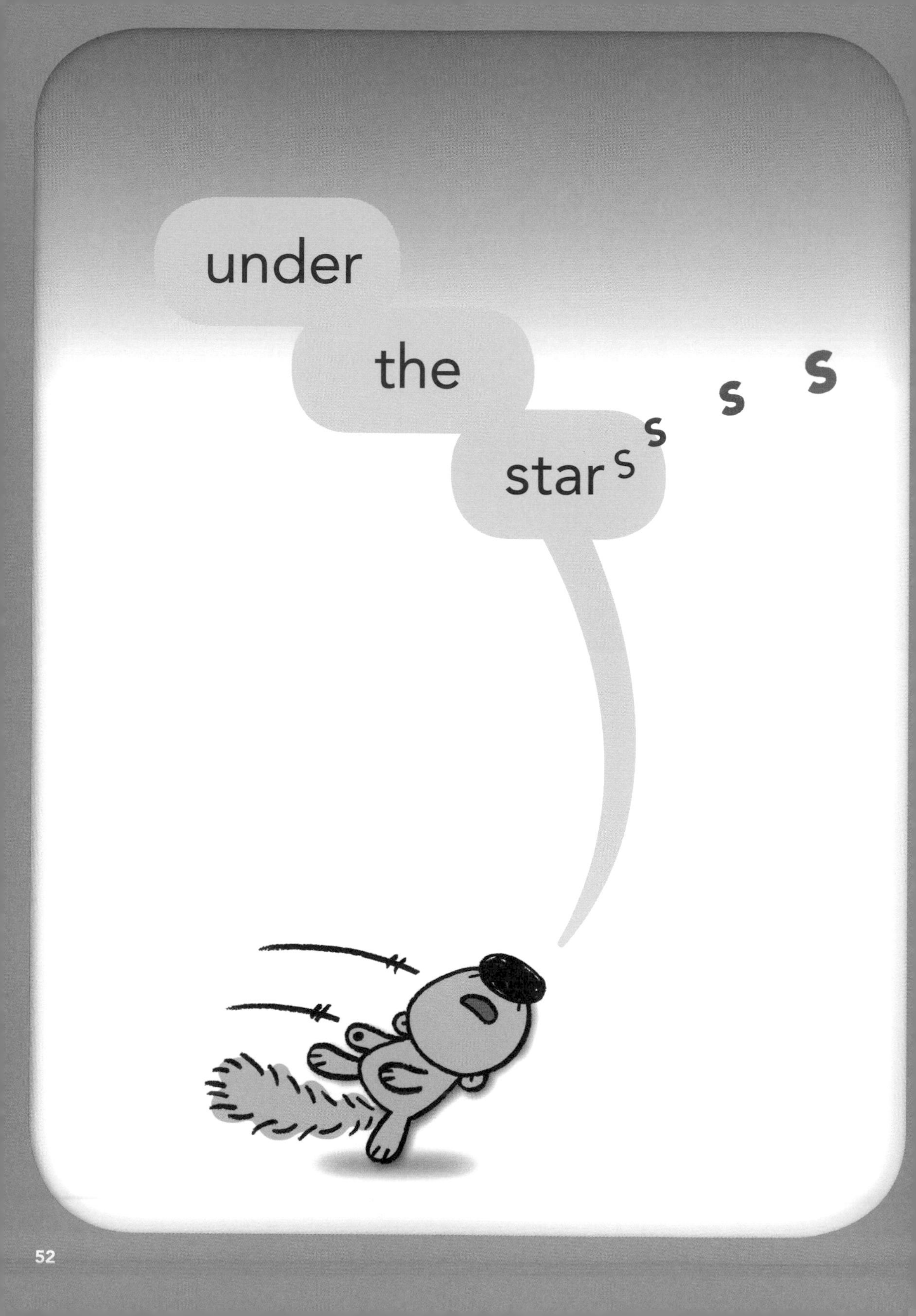
under
the
starssss

S S S S S Z Z Z Z Z Z
Plonk!

There is **something else** that Squirrels do **not** know much about. . . .

Giving up
on a friend!

I give that story **SIX STARS**!

And **one sleepy Squirrel**!

100% CORNY!

Hey-Corn!
How is the word "**asleep**" like the alphabet?

Hi-Corn!
I'm stumped. How **is** the word "asleep" like the alphabet?

They both **start** with an "**A**" and **end** with "**Z**'s"!
Har!
Hee!
Ha!
Hee!
Hee!
Har!
Har!
Ha!
Har!
Hee!
Ha!
Ha!
Har!
Ha!
That joke was **tired**!

IT'S
FUR REAL!
WITH QUIZ SQUIRREL
I am keeping it REAL— and FURRY!

Today's quiz is:
WHO SLEEPS MORE?
YAWN!
Squirrel
Armadillo
Houseplant

Who do **you** think sleeps more hours a day?

A **squirrel**?
An **armadillo**?
A **houseplant**?

Do **you** know the answer?
Say it **out loud** (and say **why**).

Then, **turn the page**!

IT'S THE ARMADILLO!
Really?
Squirrel
Houseplant

SNOOZE NEWS

Tree squirrels sleep in leafy nests in treetops and tree holes. Ground squirrels, on the other hand, snuggle down underground. The arctic ground squirrel sleeps over 16 hours a day.

The giant armadillo digs a deep hole in the dirt to sleep in. It sleeps about 18 hours a day. At night, it comes out to eat—and to dig a new hole to sleep in.

A houseplant cannot yawn or snore. But plants can behave differently during the night and day.

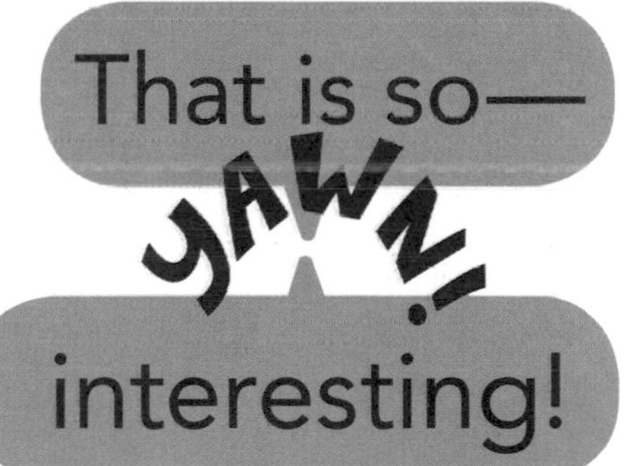

Find more **SLEEPY FACTS** at UnlimitedSquirrels.com!

Thank you, **Armadillo**!

It has been a **dream** having you on our quiz!

There is always **more** to learn when you have a **page** to turn!

Hey-Corn!
Hi-Corn!
It's ACORN-Y JOKE TIME!
93.9% CORNY!
Hey-Corn! Why are you bringing those tools to your room?
Hi-Corn! I'll tell you why!

Hee!
Ha!
I have to **MAKE MY BED**!
Ha!
Har!
Har!
Ha!
Hee!
Hee!
Har!
Hee!
Har!
Har!
Ha!
Hee!
Ha!
Har!
I **saw** that one coming. . . .

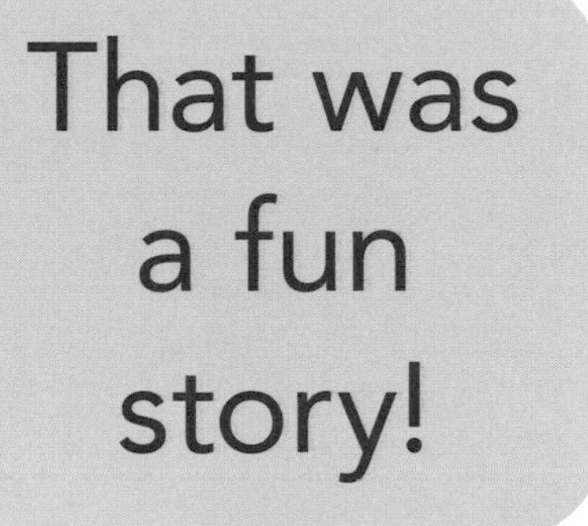
That was a fun story!
I love the night stars.
Me, too!
The BIG Story!
I Want to Sleep Under the Stars!

But **where** do the stars go during the day?

We do **not know**!

I do!

Look!

It's
Nutshell!

Squirrel
to the **Stars**!

You are
too kind.

Where do stars go during the day?

The beach?

No.

Fancy restaurants?

No.

Exclusive playgrounds?

No.

WHERE DO THEY GO!?!

Nowhere, Flappy Squirrel!

HUBBA—
WHAT!?!

Stars **do not move** around much.

We do!

Stars are **hot**.
I got the scoop!

STARS!

A STAR IS BORN

New stars are born all the time. Stars live for millions of years, and some live to be over **10 billion** years old. There are stars the size of Saturn and others that are MUCH bigger. The biggest star we know could fit billions of our sun inside it. **Talk about a big deal.**

HOT STUFF

Stars are between **5,000 and 100,000** degrees Fahrenheit. A star's color shows how hot it is. Red stars are hot. Orange and yellow are hotter. And white and blue stars are the **hottest** stars around.

I'M HOT!

STELLAR VIEWS

If you were to travel at 65 miles per hour (like driving on a highway), it would take about **163 years** to reach the sun. To visit our next-closest star, **Proxima-Centauri**, it would take almost **44 million years**. Bring snacks!

This is **fire**!

ON THE MOVE!

NO (MILKY) WAY!

There are over **100 billion** stars in our galaxy—and there could be as many as 300 billion more. **Nobody knows** how many stars there are in the whole universe, not even The Pigeon!

WOW.

HEAR! HEAR?

Is there "peace and quiet" in space? Yes! For people (and squirrels), space is mostly a **silent place**. But some astronauts say that space **smells like burnt steak**.

LOST IN SPACE

There once was a constellation of stars named the **Flying Squirrel**!

Real **big stuff**!

But if all those stars are **always there**—
Why **can't we see them** during the day?

Because of the light from **my favorite star**.

Elizabeth
Banks?

100% CORNY!

Hi-Corn!
Why was the
Sun invited to
play ball?

Hey-Corn!
I do not know.
Why was the
Sun invited to
play ball?

Ha!
Har!
Hee!
It was an **ALL-STAR** game!
Har!
Ha!
Har!
Hee!
Hee!
Hee!
Har!
Ha!
Har!
Ha!
Hee!
Pretty **bright** joke, huh?

THE TALE END!
You know what? You **Squirrels** are **like the Sun**!
Really?
How?

Well, I **look up** to you.
You are **bright**.
And—

YOU MAKE MY DAY!

We are also gassy. . . .

A BIG SQUIRRELLY THANK-YOU TO OUR EXPERTS!

Andrew Fazekas, The Night Sky Guy, author of *National Geographic Backyard Guide to the Night Sky*

Jerry Siegel, professor of Psychiatry and Biobehavioral Sciences, UCLA Center for Sleep Research

Printed in Malaysia • Reinforced binding • This book is set in Avenir LT Pro/Monotype; and Billy/Fontspring
First Edition, October 2020 • 10 9 8 7 6 5 4 3 2 1 • FAC-029191-20192

ISBN: 978-1-368-05335-8

Library of Congress Control Number: 2020931077

Visit hyperionbooksforchildren.com
and pigeonpresents.com